D1568704

For Erik

A Circle of FRIENDS

By Charlene Andersson

Illustrated by Sergio Drumond

A Circle of Friends

Copyright © 2022 by Charlene Anderson

Illustrations by Sergio Drumond

All rights reserved. No part of this book may be reproduced or transmitted in any form or by any means, electronic or mechanical, including photocopying, recording, or by any information storage and retrieval system, without written permission from the publisher. The only exception is brief quotations for reviews.

Printed and bound in the United States of America.

Erik slipped his arm into his sling, then maneuvered his backpack on his other shoulder. After a week in the hospital, it was his first day back to school since his snowboarding accident.

"I don't know why I have to go to school," he mumbled.

"The doctor said it's important to resume your normal activities," Mom said.

"I've got three pins and a screw holding my elbow together. I can't do gym or recess. And I'll have to make sure nobody bumps into me. Some normal."

Erik lumbered through the day. He did his best to avoid his friends, but David spotted him.

“Hey, bro,” said David, “how’s it going?”

“Well, I can’t do anything with this cast, so not great. But thanks for asking.”

After school, Erik plopped on the couch and watched TV.

He was miserable both in and out of school, so miserable he didn't want to do homework, chores, or even pet Harley.

A week of doing nothing passed, and Mom sat Erik down. "You may not be able to do everything you want, but there are some things you can do. You can start with taking Harley for a walk."

About to protest, Erik didn't bother. He knew Mom's 'no way' face. "Come on, Harley."

Erik walked Harley to the park. Why'd I come here? Who wants to see other kids doing things I can't? "Let's go home, boy."

"Did you have a good walk?" Mom asked.

"No." Erik went to his room and slammed the door.

Lying on his bed, Erik thought about a girl he saw at the park. She sat alone with a cast on her leg and crutches next to her.

He was still mad at life but couldn't get her out of his mind. She looked so sad.

After school the next day, Erik grabbed Harley's leash without being asked. "Come on, boy." He headed to the park, hoping to see the girl.
"Hi, I'm Erik. Looks like we have a lot in common. I crashed snowboarding. What happened to you?"

The girl looked down. “I’m Ellen. I fell down some stairs.”

“Whoa. Sorry.”

Ellen cried, and Erik’s heart sank. “It’ll be okay. Your leg will heal.”

“You don’t understand,” she said, sniffling. “We just moved here, and now it’s even harder to make friends.”

"You have a friend now," Erik said with a big smile. "I've got to go, but I'll see you tomorrow. Need help getting home?"

"No thanks. I only live a block away. I'm homeschooling for now, and my mom wants me to get out every day, so I come here."

The following day, Erik caught up with David. “Hey, want to hang out in the park after school. Maybe you can ask Rachel and Madison. I want you to meet someone.”

“Sure,” said David. “See you later.”

Erik sped-walked to the park with Harley in tow.

"Hi, Ellen," he said. About to ask how she was, David and the girls came.

"I'd like you to meet Ellen," said Erik.

After introductions, they sat and talked till almost dinner time.

As the friends were leaving to go home, a young boy fell off his bike. “Are you okay?” asked Erik.

“I think I hurt my knee.”

Erik helped the boy up. “I saw you practicing tricks. It’s super-important to wear knee and elbow pads.”

"Thanks," said the boy. "My parents could only afford the helmet."

"I'll be here tomorrow," said Erik. "I can give you some tips. I'm a bike racer."

The boy's brows rose. "Cool. I'll be here."

Erik rummaged through the garage when he got home, looking for the biking equipment he outgrew. It wasn't an easy task with only one arm, but he finally found elbow and knee pads. "Perfect."

The following day, Erik raced home from school and shoved the protective pads in his backpack. "I'm taking Harley to the park, Mom."

"Hey, boy, what do you think of our new friends? I don't know why, but I feel good helping them."

Harley just barked.

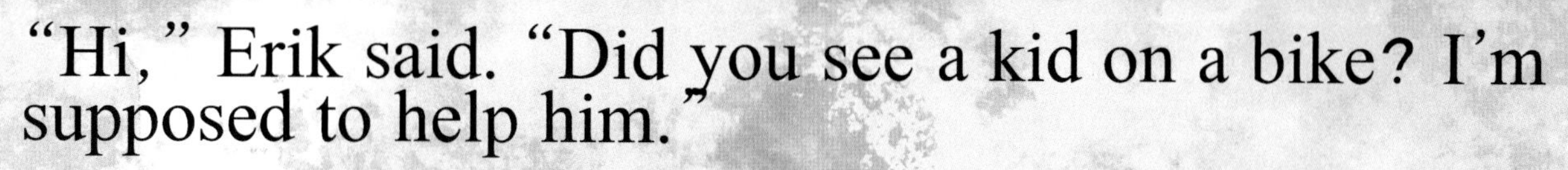

"Hi," Erik said. "Did you see a kid on a bike? I'm supposed to help him."

Ellen laughed. "You're helping someone else?"

"I guess," Erik said with a shrug… and a smile.

"HEY!" yelled the boy as he rode toward Erik.

Harley's tail wagged.

"Glad to see you," said Erik. "I had these in my garage. I'm glad they'll be put to use again. Oh, I'm Erik, and this is Ellen."

"Whoa! Thanks! I'm Ryan."

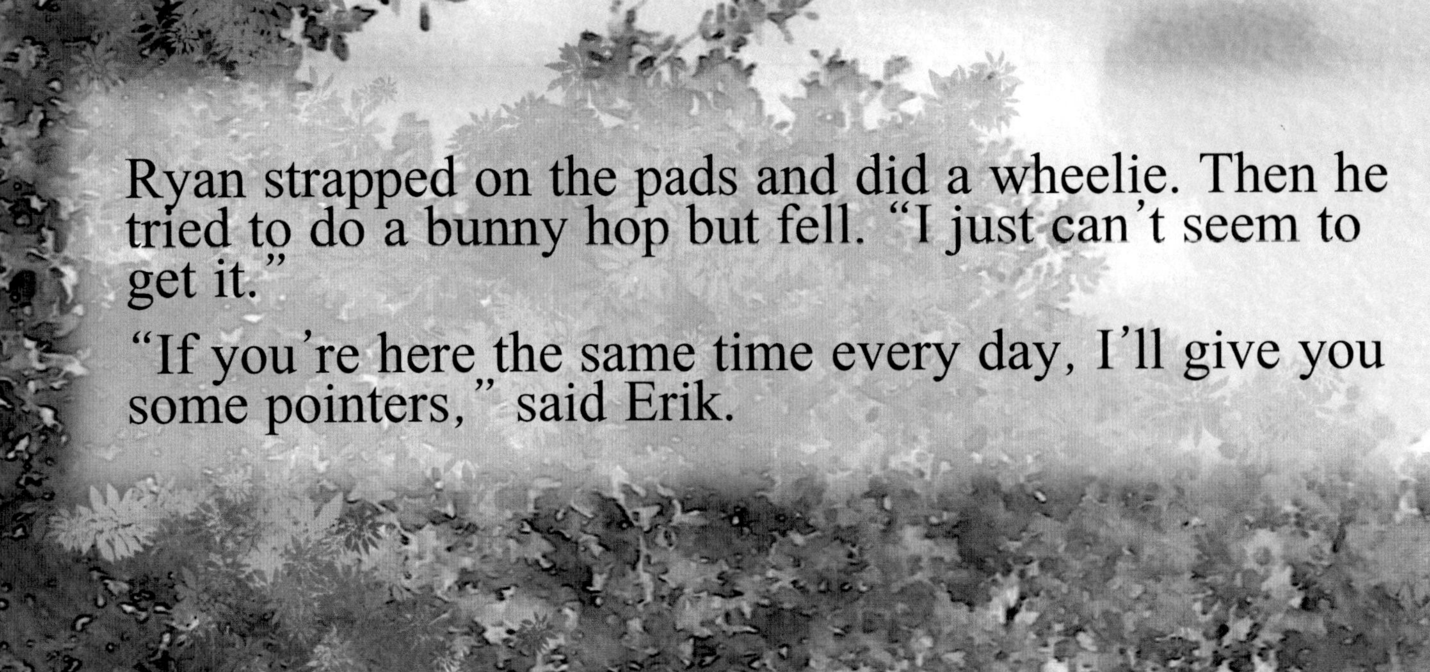

Ryan strapped on the pads and did a wheelie. Then he tried to do a bunny hop but fell. “I just can’t seem to get it.”

“If you’re here the same time every day, I’ll give you some pointers,” said Erik.

For the next few days, Erik helped Ryan. Pretty soon, other kids gathered around and asked for help.

"I should start calling you Coach Erik," said Ellen with a laugh.

After coaching the boys for a week, Erik sat with Ellen. “You know, I was miserable a week ago. All I thought about was how I couldn’t do anything. Now, I think about how I can help other people.”

“You’re a natural at it,” said Ellen. “I’m glad we met.”

"I'm glad we met too," said Erik with his easy smile.

"Hey," called David walking toward Erik and Ellen.

"Hi," called Rachel and Madison.

"Since it's Friday, want to go to the movies?" asked David.

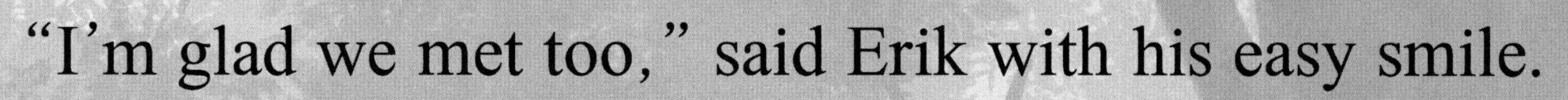

"Hey, that's a great idea," said Erik.

"Thanks for including me!" said Ellen. "I forgot my phone; I'll have to go home and ask."

"That's fine," said Madison. "The movie doesn't start for an hour."

"We'll walk you," said Erik. He handed Harley's leash to David, then helped Ellen up.

A feeling of happiness grew inside Erik. Who knew helping others could make me feel so good!

About the Author

Charlene Andersson has been a teacher for several decades and she lectures extensively on the topic of effective teaching both on the academic side and the emotional side. Charlene believes strongly that education and growing up is not only the child's responsibility but also the parents. For the parents have to be the strongest advocate for their children. Charlene was chosen to consult internationally on curriculum and the emotional issues children face in elementary school. She understands that when a child's self image is compromised, regardless of what is being taught, it is difficult for the child to embrace the teaching. Charlene hopes that this book helps both children and parents identify these common pitfalls that every child will travel through in their journey to adulthood.

Charlene currently lives in Los Angeles with her family. In her free time she enjoys the beach and spending time with her adult children!